# PAUL KROPP

# MICRO
# MAN

EMC Publishing, St. Paul, Minnesota

**Encounters Series** Titles

| | | | |
|---|---|---|---|
| Burn Out | Dead On | Gang War | Micro Man |
| Dope Deal | Dirt Bike | Wild One | The Beast |
| Runaway | No Way | Snow Ghost | Spin Out |
| Hot Cars | Fair Play | Baby Baby | Amy's Wish |

**Encounters Series** Teacher's Guides are also available.

**Library of Congress Cataloging in Publication Data**

Kropp, Paul.
  Micro man.

  (Encounters series)
  Summary: Micro Man and his buddy, Rob, try to find out
who is tampering with the school's computers and funds.
  [1. Mystery and detective stories. 2. Computers—Fiction]
I. Title. II. Series.

PZ7.K93Mi  1986  [Fic]                           85-6947
ISBN 0-8219-0162-1

Published by EMC Publishing
300 York Avenue
St. Paul, Minnesota 55101

Printed in Singapore
0  9  8  7  6  5  4  3  2  1

# CONTENTS

# CHAPTER

**1**

I could have told you that it was going to be a bad, bad day. I knew that my computer grade would be rotten. I knew that some of my football buddies would give me a hard time. I even had a hunch that something really big would go wrong.

What I didn't know, then, was how rotten things were going to get.

Before I saw my midterm grade in computers, I thought I could handle it. That just shows how much I know. I thought my mark would be low, but still passing. Maybe a 55 or so. But then the bad news came out of the printer—a 38. I'd flunked!

"That's the pits, Rob," I heard Micro Man say. "You should have done better than that."

Micro seemed more interested in my mark than he was in his own. Of course, his marks were so high up in space that he had no reason to worry about them. The only reason he didn't get 100 in computers was that Old Mrs. Connor caught him playing Plato's Cave. Plato's Cave was a game that Micro had made up himself. He was that smart.

And I was that dumb. Maybe my father was right when he said I'd always be a dumb jock. I could hardly wait to see the I-told-you-so look on his face when I told him. Then I'd get one more lousy lecture about Eric, the smart kid next door. And me, the stupid kid who plays football.

I pulled my grade sheet out of the printer and crumpled it into a ball.

"Don't give up so fast," Micro said. He grabbed the ball of paper before I had a chance to throw it away. "Let's check the marks."

6

"Computers don't make mistakes," I told him.

"Yeah, but people do," Micro said. "I think Mrs. Connor must have made an input error."

"Speak English," I said.

"Maybe Connor typed in the wrong numbers," Micro explained. He shook his head as if he were talking to some guy with brain damage. I was about to tell him that I didn't need any more put-downs, but then Mrs. Connor came blasting in.

"All right, take your seats. I want to

go over the midterm grades," Connor shouted.

We all sat down at our desks. Mrs. Connor stared at us until the room was quiet. She was one of *those* teachers.

Connor went through all the garbage about grades and how her program figured out the midterm. She kept saying things like, "Don't give up just because you got a low grade this time." I felt like she looked at me each time she said that.

"I was pleased to see that some of you did so well," Connor said. "We all knew that Mark would be close to perfect," she said, looking at Micro Man, "but some of the rest of you really surprised me."

Buggsy Crawford followed that up with a whisper that could be heard all over the class. "Nick got 92!" From the look on Nick's face, it had to be true.

The class went wild as the word spread around. Nick Bistas aces the course! Who could believe it? Yet Nick was grinning like he'd just scored a big touchdown with two seconds left to play.

"All right, quiet down," Old Mrs. Connor said. "Nick did very well and that should be a lesson to all of you. It shows the kind of grade you can get if you really get down to work."

"Nick never worked a day in his whole life," I whispered to Micro. "Something stinks."

Micro nodded. Neither of us much liked Nick, but Micro had more reasons than I did. It all went back to sixth grade. That's when Nick tried to turn Micro's face into lumpy pudding. Nick didn't get too far in that, but Micro got the message. Not long after that, Micro began to lift weights. Now he had more muscles than any kid on the football team. He must be the only whiz kid in the world who can press 100 pounds.

I sat through Connor's class feeling like I was really dumb. I mean, if Nick could get a 92 and Micro a 97, then what was wrong with me?

When Connor was done talking, she said we could have the last few minutes of class to work on our programs. That meant we could finally talk.

Micro turned to me. "Rob, what did you get on that long program I helped you with?"

"I can't remember. It was a good grade, though, maybe a 70."

"This computer grade sheet says you only got a 44 on it. Let's check the grade Mrs. Connor put on the project itself."

"I haven't got it," I said. "I must have lost it or something." I'd never been able to hold on to a notebook for more than two months in my entire life.

"You're hopeless," Micro Man said.

"Worse—I'm a failure," I sighed.

That's what I felt like—and that's what my father would say. I had worked my brains into mush on the computer course and only got a 38. Maybe it was time to give up. I had an awful feeling in my stomach when I thought about all that work down the drain.

"Maybe Connor can check her grade book," Micro went on. I wondered if he was just trying to cheer me up.

"Oh, forget it," I told him. "Maybe I can pull the grade up next term. My parents will ground me for sure, so I should have plenty of time to study. It's a good thing football season is over or I'd get pulled from the team."

"You shouldn't take a grade like this

without checking," Micro said.

I was going to answer, "What's the use," when Nick came over to my desk.

"How'd you do, Rob?" he asked me, a sick smile plastered on his face. I knew perfectly well that he knew.

"The pits," I answered. I was trying very hard to smile back.

"It's lucky you don't have to be good at computers to be captain of the football team, eh?" he said. He smiled as if it were a joke. But I knew very well what was behind it. Nick had run against me for team captain—and lost. Ever since

then he'd been searching for ways to make me look bad.

Micro spoke up just then. "Nick, why don't you leave Rob alone and go pop a pimple, will you?"

Nick shot an angry look at the two of us and went back to his desk.

His leaving didn't matter much to me. I was so far down in the dumps that I thought I had to be at the bottom.

But I was wrong. The dumps were a lot deeper than I thought. I didn't find that out until the end of the class when the PA called out my name.

*Rob Denby report to the office, please. Rob Denby to the office....*

# CHAPTER

# 2

For most kids, being called to the office means trouble. But not for me. I don't skip classes or come in late or goof around in the lunch room. I may be dumb in computers, but I'm not stupid.

Ever since I was voted captain of the football team, I've seen the office in a new way. When we ran a dance to make some money, the guys in the office were really on our side. Now I know the principal so well I can almost call her by her first name. Well, almost.

"Hi, Mrs. Varey," I said as I came into her office. I felt much better just

being out of the computer room.

"Rob, I've got to talk to you," she said. "It's serious."

That was the first clue that things were going to get even worse for me. The second clue was when I saw the office curtains. In our school, the principal's office has big glass walls. When nothing serious is going on, the curtains are open. When some kid is getting chewed out for something, the curtains are closed.

And the curtains were closed.

"Rob, you'd better sit down," Mrs. Varey told me.

"What's the matter," I asked her. The last time I was in her office, everything was great. Our dance had made over a thousand dollars. The Rotary Club and the Board would both match what we made on the dance. That gave us over $3000 to buy new team uniforms. Back then, Mrs. Varey said I was a hero for making the whole thing work. And even my father had to admit that I did a good job.

Now Mrs. Varey looked at me like I was some kind of rat.

"Rob, didn't you tell me that the

school made about $1200 on that football team dance?" she asked.

"That's right. It was $1258 and some change. I did the figures myself and Micro Man—uh, Mark Sanders—he checked them."

"So you're sure there wasn't a mistake," she asked.

"Well, if it was just me ...," I said, smiling. "But Mark hasn't made a mistake since, uh, I think it was five years ago."

The principal smiled and shook her head. I still didn't know what she was getting at.

"Rob, I believed those figures you gave me. In fact, I've got checks from the Rotary and the Seattle Board here on my desk. But today Mrs. Connor brought me the student council figures from the computer. She says that your profit is much, much less than what you told me."

"How much less?" I asked. I was sweating now and I didn't even know why.

"A thousand dollars less," Mrs. Varey said. "Mrs. Connor has checked the figures three times and I've been through them once. You only made $258.76 on that dance, Rob."

"No way," I said.

"Computers don't make mistakes," the principal said. That seemed to be the line for the day. "And even if they do, the bank figures would show the error."

"But that's crazy," I said. "You were at the dance. We had five hundred kids there at three bucks a person. The band gave back their fee, so they didn't cost anything. We made some extra money selling pop and checking coats. You can take away the costs of cleaning and police, but we had to make over a thousand. It was the best dance we ever had at this school."

"I know that, Rob. When you said $1200 was the profit, I didn't doubt you at all. But now I have these figures from the computer.... Well, I don't know what to think."

She handed me the computer print-out. I was too upset even to look at it.

"Rob," Mrs. Varey went on, "we should have made more money on that dance, but something seems to have gone wrong. I have to know what happened—

and soon. If we can't get this cleared up in a week, I'll have to return these checks from the Board and the Rotary Club. Then we might as well forget about new uniforms."

"But Mrs. Varey—" I said, not sure what else I could tell her at this point.

"The point is, Rob, that I have to know what happened to the dance money. Right now, the computer is against you and the bank is against you. I want to believe you, but there's a lot of money at stake. I have to know what went wrong."

"But nothing did go wrong. I'll have Micro go through all the figures. I'm certain it's just a simple mistake someplace."

"I can give you until the start of next week, Rob. If the money doesn't turn up by then, I won't have any choice. I'll have to return these checks. And then I'll have to explain what happened to your team and the other kids who worked on the dance."

I began to picture what all of them would do to me. I wondered how many of my bones would end up broken. I wondered what my nose would look like smashed into my face.

"Of course, I think we'll have it all sorted out before then," Mrs. Varey went on. She seemed more hopeful than I was.

"Yes...er, of course," I said, too confused to know what I was saying.

I stumbled out of the principal's office and into the cool air of the hall outside. Micro Man was waiting for me.

"What's the matter?" he asked. "You look like you died and didn't quite make it to heaven."

"I'd be better off dead," I told him. I wondered, right then, if it had been a

smart move of mine ever to be born. "You know the dance we ran for the football team?"

"Yeah. Best thing you ever did, given your somewhat limited brain power," he told me.

"We're a thousand dollars short!" I whispered to him.

Micro got a look on his face that I hadn't seen before. I think, for just a second, he felt dumb.

# CHAPTER
# 3

We couldn't talk right away about the missing money. For one thing, Mr. Van Woort, the school janitor, kept trying to sweep the floor under my feet.

For another, all the people in the office were staring at us. I wondered if they knew.

"Meet me in the weight room after last hour," Micro said.

"In the weight room?" I asked. "Look, we're in real trouble."

"That's why I'm going to lift weights," he answered. "It helps to calm me down. Besides, no one ever goes there except me, so it'll be a good place to talk."

I handed him the computer printout that Mrs. Varey and given me. Then I went off to spend the rest of the day worrying. I saw myself in the Seattle jail. I saw myself turned into hamburger by the football team. I tried to see some hope, someplace, anyplace. But I couldn't. All I could see was my father's face and the way he'd look at me when the news came out.

Micro was already pressing some weights when I got to the weight room behind the school gym.

"What kept you?" he asked.

"I ran into Animal on the way down and he wanted to talk." Animal was the name we gave last year to Melvin Weiner. He was so big and hairy that I think his parents must have been apes.

"What did he want?" Micro asked. He was lying on a bench, holding an 80-pound weight over his chest. He held it up as if it weighed less than a loaf of bread.

"The usual stuff. If the uniforms don't get here by next month, he says I'd better move to Alaska. For my health."

"Don't buy—" Micro said, lifting the weight again,"—your plane ticket yet." Then he lowered the weight down on the stand. "I think I've got an answer."

"Sometimes, Micro, I really have to hand it to you."

"Don't hand me anything just yet. I haven't got the money or the person who took it. Here, Rob, see if you can press 40 pounds," he said.

"My whole future is on the line and you want me to lift weights?"

Sometimes Micro Man can be really strange.

"Well, for one thing, weight lifting is good for you when you're under stress—like right now. And you may need some real muscle when Animal and the rest of your football team come after you."

"I thought you had an answer," I said.

"Yeah, but not to the big question. Look, the whole thing is simple. The student council bank account is short by a thousand dollars. Our dance figures on the computer have been changed so that they come up short by a thousand dollars."

"So?" I asked—or grunted. Playing

football is one thing, lifting weights is something else.

"So the principal wonders if you—or maybe even I—have that thousand dollars hidden away some place," Micro said.

"But we don't," I grunted.

"Right. And if we did, we'd have to waste it on plane tickets to Alaska.

"Well, what good is all that?" I asked, putting the weight down. "All you can prove is that *we* are the likely suspects. I don't need a high IQ to figure that out."

"Right again, Rob. All we really know is this . . . One—we didn't take the money.

Two—whoever did take it can beat the school computer."

"And three," I said, "unless we can count up a few more facts, I'll be dead. There's got to be something else." That sinking feeling was coming back again.

"Well, we do have Nick's 92 in computer class. There's something pretty strange about that."

"But it doesn't help us unless Nick's got a thousand dollars in his back pocket."

"That's true—but it is strange. And here's something else. Not only does Old Mrs. Connor know how to use the school computer, she also puts money in the bank for the student council."

"And she doesn't like me."

"Connor doesn't like anyone. You might be right about one thing, though."

"What's that?"

"That whoever took the money doesn't like you and wants to make it look like you did it. But...."

"But what?" I asked.

"But, then again, maybe not."

"Micro," I said, "you're going to drive me nuts. I've got four days to find out what happened to the missing money and get the person who stole it. If I can't, then I'm up the old creek with no paddle."

"You didn't tell me about the four days," Micro said.

"Yeah, Varey said she'd tell the team about the whole mess next Monday. Next Tuesday you'll find parts of my body scattered all over the schoolyard."

"Could be messy," Micro noted.

"And painful," I told him. "What am I going to do?"

"I think the first thing is to stop talking about this thing as only your problem. We're in this together. Besides, if you get blamed for the loss, people will think I was the brains behind it all."

"You're so modest, Micro."

"Yeah," he admitted, "but I'm also stumped." There was a funny look on his face. Maybe this was the first time he'd been stumped since Nick Bistas beat him up in the school playground.

"There's got to be a clue of some kind," I said to Micro. "What do the cops look for, anyway? It's not the sort of thing where they dust for fingerprints...."

Micro looked down at me and smiled.

"That's it," he said. "In your own stupid way, you may have got us going on the right track."

"How?" I asked him.

"With a fingerprint!"

# CHAPTER
# 4

Fingerprints might make some sense if this were a murder story and the body were still warm on the floor. They might make sense if this were a jewel theft and the robbers had just left. But this was a computer crime and no one knew when it took place.

What did Micro have in mind? You can't put fingerprint powder on a computer screen.

Micro, of course, wouldn't explain. When he gets an idea in his head, he just runs with it. He keeps on running until he gets the answer he wants. In this case,

I needed the answer more than he did. If Micro couldn't come up with one, I'd be wading in trouble up to my knees. That is, if I had any knees left when the football team got through with me.

"Where are we going?" I asked. I was standing in the locker room while he threw his clothes on.

"To find fingerprints," was all he said. I wondered if his brains had exploded at last. Maybe there's only so much you can pack in.

I followed Micro up to the library. It was open, as always, and Cheryl Hodder was working at the desk. I had once tried to go out with her, but that's a whole other story—and not a very happy one.

Micro waved to Cheryl and went right to the computer at the back. He sat down and stared at the keyboard. For a moment, I thought he might really be looking for fingerprints. But that's dumb. He was just taking some time to think.

"What are you doing?" I asked him.

"Need a program," he said.

"Huh?"

"Got to break the code."

"Huh?"

31

"First I need to break into the system."

I finally woke up to the fact that Micro was talking to himself more than to me. There wasn't much I could do to help him on the machine. There wasn't much anyone could do to help Micro with a computer. So I kept an eye out to make sure that no one was spying on us. I wasn't sure what Micro was doing, but I had a hunch it might get us in trouble. And more trouble I didn't need.

"O.K., now we just wait and see if it'll break in," Micro said. This time he was whispering to me.

"So now can you explain?"

"Sure," he said. "All the school computers are hooked up to each other. What I'm trying to do is get into the student council file and see what happened to the thousand dollars."

"I knew what you were doing wasn't legal. Look, I don't think I can handle any more trouble today."

"Don't worry about it—I'll be in that file in no time at all."

"But you can't just bust into that kind of stuff. Connor wouldn't leave that wide open so just anybody could get at it."

"Right. I see you did learn something in computer class. Old Mrs. Connor would put a code on the file to keep people out of it. The code, of course, is a secret. But if I can break the code, then I can get into the file easily," Micro said.

"So how are you planning to break the secret code?" I asked him.

"Not so loud, Rob. Pretend that we're just playing a game or something—just in case Cheryl has big ears."

I looked over at Cheryl and it seemed to me that her ears were just fine. It seemed to me, in fact, that most of Cheryl was just fine. But that's part of the other story.

"This is what I'm doing," Micro went on. "I've made a program for the computer to try out all the possible codes until it finds the right one. It's like trying to open a lock by trying each number until you hit the right one."

"But that'll take years," I said.

"The computer is a lot faster than we are. Give it two minutes," Micro said.

And he was right. The student council file came up on the screen.

"Can you break into anything like that?" I asked.

"No. A good program would have a better code system. But I figured that Mrs. Connor couldn't write a good program to save her life. Some day I'll have to show her how to protect the files."

As I said, what I like about Micro is that he's so modest.

"What are you looking for now?" I asked.

"A fingerprint," he said, though that didn't mean much to me.

I looked up to see Cheryl walking over toward us. I figured I had better head her off. That way Micro could keep on looking for ... uh, fingerprints.

"Say, Cheryl, could you help me find a book? I've been looking for that new novel by...."

"Rob, who are you trying to kid? Football players don't read," Cheryl said with a laugh.

She sounded just like my father.

"As a matter of fact," I told her, "I've read quite a few books this year."

"Yeah, comic books. What is Micro up to?" she asked, looking over my shoulder at him.

"I, uh, he's just trying out a new program," I said, and that much was true.

"I'm supposed to keep an eye on who uses the machine," she said. "The librarian thinks that someone is using it to mess up her overdue files."

"Some people have no respect," I said.

"Yeah. I think that Mr. Van Woort is doing it. Did you know that he takes a computer course at night school?"

"Maybe he wants to program his

broom," I said. Micro was taking his own sweet time while I tried to stall Cheryl.

"I think computers are boring," she said, drawing out the "o" to show just how boring they were.

"I guess you didn't help Nick get his 92 in computers, then," I said. It bothered me that she had turned me down and then started going out with Nick Bistas. I guess some people have no taste.

"Nick doesn't need my help for anything," she said. "But I hear you're going to need lots of help real soon."

"How's that?" Micro was still staring at the computer screen.

"I hear that something has gone wrong with the football uniform deal," Cheryl said.

"Oh, where did you hear that?" I asked, starting to sweat.

"Just a rumor, you know. But you better not blow the uniform money, Rob. A lot of people put a lot of work into that dance. We expect to see something for it. Nick would go crazy if anything went wrong."

"I can just bet," I said, though Nick wasn't nearly as scary as Animal. In a

fight, I might even have a chance against Nick.

"What's Micro doing on the machine?" she asked, looking over at him.

"Oh, nothing," I said, trying to stall a few minutes more. But I guess I had held her back about as long as I could. She walked quickly over to the computer.

"What's this?" she asked, looking closely at the screen.

"Just a new game I made up," Micro told her, calm as could be. "I call it Plato's Cave 2.0. You try to find your way out of a cave into the real world."

I looked on the screen and there it was—a game. There was a picture of a cave with a little man trying to find his way out.

"I guess you really must be a genius," Cheryl said, shaking her head and walking away. With her gone, I could find out what Micro was really up to.

"Did you find it?" I whispered to him.

"Find what?" he asked, smiling from one large ear to the other.

"What you wanted—the fingerprint."

"Yeah," he said. He seemed so busy playing his new game that he wasn't worried about the money any more.

"So what did you find?"

"Only one fingerprint," he said, "and I think it belongs to Old Mrs. Connor."

# CHAPTER
# 5

I better explain the fingerprint. Micro told me that some computers leave a fingerprint just like people can. When someone goes into a computer file, the person has to use a keyboard. Each keyboard has a number. That number could tell us what keyboard was used to break into the file. Micro was looking for the fingerprint of the keyboard that was used to change the dance money. And he found it.

The real figures had been changed the day after we sent them in. And the fingerprint came from the teacher's keyboard in Mrs. Connor's room.

"So Connor did it," I said to Micro. We were on the way to his house on Meadowlands.

"No, someone on Mrs. Connor's machine did it. All I have is the number and the date when it was done. It might have been Connor on the keyboard, or it might have been someone else. We have a suspect, but no proof."

"Great."

"If it makes you feel better, I think we can start to narrow down the suspects," Micro said.

"Will that stop Animal and the rest of them from beating me up?"

"Not until we find the thousand dollars. What we haven't got is the hacker who's behind all this."

"Hacker?"

"A hacker is a crazy who has fun breaking into some other person's program."

"Someone just like you," I said, making fun of him.

"Not quite," Micro said. "I'm a programmer. A hacker is someone who knows enough to break into a file, but can't cover up what's been done."

"So how do we catch this hacker?"

"We just tap into Connor's computer and see if anyone goes into the student council file—and then we've got our man."

"Or woman," I said, thinking of Old Mrs. Connor. "But, tell me this—what if the hacker doesn't come back on? The guy has already got a thousand dollars. Maybe that's enough."

"A hacker can't control himself. Now that he's been in the file once, he'll be back."

"Like returning to the scene of the crime," I said.

"That makes it sound corny—but I guess you're right. You better hope that the hacker comes back in the next four days. If he doesn't, we're up that old creek—"

"With no paddle," I said. All I could picture was Animal and his friends as they turned me into playdough.

The next day, I looked at Mrs. Connor with new eyes. I had never liked her very much. Now I knew why. She has very small, shifty eyes and there was something funny about the way she acted. It was as if her mind were off someplace else. Maybe she was worried about getting caught. When she looked over at me, I was sure that she was feeling guilty. Maybe she was hard up for money. Maybe she wanted some extra cash for a face-lift. But did she have to throw the blame on me? That's pretty low—even for a teacher.

Micro kept his home computer hooked into the school system all the time. This didn't tell us much during the day. But we knew that the hacker wouldn't risk getting caught on school time. We figured the real action would be after school. That's when the hacker could come in and do what she wanted. That's when Mrs. Connor could take all the time in the world to cover up her crime.

So we waited at Micro's house and watched his computer.

And we waited.

We had four days.

On Thursday, we waited by the computer for eight hours. At first we watched the screen, but then that got boring so we played cards. Micro lifted

weights and I cleaned out the food in the fridge. And we talked.

"Maybe the hacker went out on a date," I said when it was getting close to midnight.

"Hackers don't have dates," Micro shot back.

"Then what do they do?"

"They make out with disk drives," he said, smiling. "By the way, have you told your father about your grade in the computer course?"

"I thought I'd be better off waiting until the report card came in the mail," I told him. "He thinks I'm pretty stupid as it is."

"Your dad expects a lot from you, I guess."

"Yeah. I think he wanted some kind of genius for a son, but he got me."

"You're pretty smart in some things, Rob, and the kids at school look up to you. You shouldn't put yourself down all the time."

"Maybe you're right. You see, my father keeps on comparing me to this kid Eric Weiner next door. Weiner is a real whiz kid."

"Is that Animal's brother?" Micro asked.

"Yeah, I guess he got all the brains while Animal got all the muscle. I didn't get much of either."

"Or maybe you got a little bit of both," Micro said. "Go home, get some sleep, and we'll catch our hacker tomorrow."

On Friday, I felt a little better, but time was running out. We had only three days left to catch the hacker. And I wasn't sure what we'd do if we did catch the person. I wondered if Micro had really thought this whole thing through.

"What do we do if the hacker breaks into the file again?" I asked him.

"Then we go catch the guy in the act," Micro said.

"What does that mean?"

"Well," Micro said after a while, "we go tell the person that we've caught him and tell him to come clean. We pretend that we know all about what's been done."

"Do we?"

"Not really. But whoever it is will still have a lot of explaining to do. The guy might confess right on the spot."

"Yeah, but what if the guy doesn't?"

"Then we . . . I don't really know," Micro said.

"In the movies they always confess on the spot," I said, trying to look on the bright side.

"Yeah, in the movies."

We were both quiet for a while. I was worried about what would happen to me on Monday. I wondered if the principal would call the whole football team together and give them the bad news, or tell them one at a time. I guess it didn't matter much. Nick and Animal would get the guys together and come after me. Maybe I could have one last lunch in the cafeteria before they got me. Then again, maybe not. Maybe it would be better to get beaten up than to face all the kids who worked on the dance. Talk about disgrace!

Micro looked as upset as I was. He didn't talk about it, but he was in trouble too. No one would think I had enough brains to steal the money. Micro would be sure to get blamed. Maybe the football team wouldn't go after him. But he'd still be in real trouble. It might be the first time a 90+ student was ever kicked out of high school. Even tapping into the school system, like we were doing, was against the law. In a funny way, Micro had more to lose than I did. They might trash up my body—but this might cost Micro his whole future.

I was just getting hungry for dinner when the computer screen flashed.

"Is that it?" I asked him.

"Someone is on Connor's keyboard," Micro said. He went and punched some numbers into his machine. The screen filled with the student council file.

"And the hacker is playing with student council money," he said.

"We've got the guy," I yelled. "And I just bet its Old Mrs. Connor."

# CHAPTER 6

We got to school in five minutes flat. Micro drove like a wild man. I think he even beat the record that Buggsy Crawford set last year in his souped-up Chevy SS.

The school was still open when we got there. Night school hadn't started yet, but there were some people waiting by the gym and the pool. The halls on the second floor were empty.

Micro and I ran all the way to the computer room. Then we stopped, just outside the door. Micro looked quickly through the little window in the door. He

nodded and I took my turn at the window. Then we both knew that we'd caught our man—or woman!

It was Old Mrs. Connor.

I gave Micro one of my I-knew-it-all-the-time smiles. Then I turned the handle and we walked inside.

Mrs. Connor looked up from the computer and stared at us. Something about that stare just knocked the boldness right out of me.

I looked at Micro, hoping that he would say something. But he seemed at a loss for words. It must have been the first time ever that Micro didn't know what to say.

Of course, neither did I.

"Well, what brings you two here?" Connor asked.

I knew she was guilty. I could tell by the way she acted, the way she tried to pretend everything was O.K. But what should we do now?

"We, uh, we know what you're up to, Mrs. Connor," I said. I got the feeling that this wouldn't be as easy as it was in the movies. She was cool—too cool.

"Don't bother to clear the screen. We

already know what you're doing," I said.
I wasn't sure if that was true or not, but
that line was Micro Man's idea.

Micro just stood there. His mouth was
open and he looked like a nerd.

"You'll lose your teaching job for this,"
I said. "But if you come clean now, you
might be able to stay out of jail." I was
feeling stronger now, like the good guy
on a TV crime show.

"Jail?" Mrs. Connor asked. "What are
you talking about, Rob?"

Micro was looking at me, shaking his
head. He was trying to tell me to shut

up, but I didn't know this at the time. I just went ahead and put the other foot in my mouth.

"We know that you're playing with the student council accounts, Mrs. Connor. You might as well admit the whole thing to us."

Mrs. Connor was looking at me as if I had escaped from some mental hospital.

"Mark, what on earth is Rob talking about?" she asked.

"We must have made a mistake, Mrs. Connor," Micro said.

"We did?" That sinking feeling came back to me in a rush, only worse than before.

"We did," Micro told me. "You see, someone has been changing figures in the school accounts...."

"You're quite right," Mrs. Connor said. "Your friend here is short a thousand dollars on that dance. I was just checking through the figures here to see if it was placed in the wrong account. But I haven't found any mistake yet."

"You won't find a mistake," I told her. "Micro checked the files two days ago. The money was stolen—and it was stolen by a hacker using your machine."

"But how—?"

"We checked back in the file," I told her. I looked over at Micro to see if he wanted to explain, but he was just looking at the ceiling.

"But to do that you need the code. I'm the only person who knows that," Mrs. Connor said.

"Micro made a program to figure it out," I said, bragging.

"I guess there's no sense hiding it," Micro began. "Rob already told you we got into the file. In fact, your code was quite easy to break. It only took about two minutes for my program to do it. But the point is that someone had broken it before me. And that someone stole the football team money."

"So you just broke into the file, eh?" asked Mrs. Connor. She wasn't smiling.

"We had to break in, Mrs. Connor," Micro said. "I know it's wrong, but we were just trying to figure out who stole the money. I can even tell you just when the money was moved and how it was done. The only thing I don't know is who did it."

"So that's why you two came rushing in here like cops-and-robbers. You thought that I—" And then she began to get angry. "You thought that I stole the money."

"I guess we were wrong," I said.

I had this urge to shrink into my shoes.

"You bet you were wrong, young man. And you, Mark, have broken into the school computer files. You're smart enough to know how serious that is. How do I know that you two haven't been trying to cover up your own crime?"

"We didn't take any money," Micro told her.

"We were just trying to catch the guy who did it," I added. "There's someone in this school who's taken a thousand dollars and all the blame is on me."

"Maybe that's where the blame should be," Mrs. Connor said. "I want to see both of you in the principal's office on Monday. You've got a lot of explaining to do ... and not just to the school. I'm going to bring the police in on this."

"But Mrs. Connor—" I said.

"I've got to teach my night school class in a few minutes. You two can save what you have to say until Monday. The principal and the police will want to hear a good story."

# CHAPTER 7

"Well, you were close, but no cigar," I told Micro as we walked down the hall. I knew that we were worse off now than we were before. But I didn't want to say that out loud.

"I hate cigars anyhow," Micro said. I could tell he felt pretty bad.

"I shouldn't have told Mrs. Connor about getting in the files," I told him. "That just got us in more trouble."

"It's still no reason for her to bring in the police," Micro said.

"Maybe it's just a threat," I told him.

"Old Mrs. Connor doesn't make

threats. By Tuesday, all of Seattle will know about it."

"Yeah, we'll make the *Times*. TOP STUDENT KICKED OUT FOR COMPUTER CRIME—it'll make a nice headline," I said.

"Make that TOP STUDENT AND FOOTBALL CAPTAIN KICKED OUT," Micro added. "I wonder if anyone will hire a computer programmer who got kicked out of twelfth grade."

"Better learn how to push a broom," I said.

"Hey, let's look on the bright side. There are worse things than going to jail."

"Like what?"

"Like my father could kick me off my computer," he said with a sigh.

"Think he would?" I asked.

"If we don't solve this thing," Micro said, "he won't even let me program my clock radio. And all you worry about is getting beaten up."

"I guess." Only Micro Man would worry more about losing his computer than getting his head punched in. I was worried too, though, and not just about my health. Once the police came in, my father would never let me live this thing down. Never.

I bought Micro a coffee from the machine in the cafeteria. The place was pretty empty now that night school had started. There were only three or four other people in the whole place. That was counting Mr. Van Woort pushing his broom by the pop machine. I tried to picture Micro doing the same job, but somehow he just didn't fit.

We sat at a table and didn't say anything for a while. I'm not sure what

Micro was thinking about. I was thinking about how the football team would tear me apart. It might be better if they beat me up so badly that I had to go to hospital. Maybe it would make my father feel sorry for me. Then again....

"Let's get this thing worked out," Micro said. His brain was working again, like a big V-8 inside a muscle car.

"So far," he said, writing this down on a piece of paper, "we have three clues. First, we know that somebody broke into the student council file and moved a thousand dollars out of it. Second, we think that somebody got into our class grades and raised Nick Bistas up to a 92."

"Are you sure about that?" I asked.

"Just guessing right now. But we both know that there's no way Nick could pull off an honest 92, right?"

"Right," I said. "What about clue number three?"

"Somebody has been playing games with the library files."

"So what?"

"So maybe nothing. I'm just trying to get the facts down right now. I don't even know if any of these connect," Micro said with a frown.

"So who are the suspects?" I asked. "We know that Old Mrs. Connor didn't do it."

"No—all we know for sure is that Connor wasn't stealing anything *tonight.* Now, it doesn't make much sense for her to grab a thousand dollars when she could get blamed for it. But who knows? Maybe it was just a practice run for some time when she wants a lot of money."

"You really think so?"

"Nah, Mrs. Connor's not smart enough to pull off a big computer crime."

"But she's the teacher," I said.

"She's just not smart enough," Micro told me. He looked at me as if I was quite a way below even Mrs. Connor.

"So who else is there?"

"Well, there's you, me, Connor, Nick Bistas—"

"He hasn't got two brains to rub together," I said.

"But he might have a friend who could give him some help. Also, Nick would just love to throw the blame on

you. He's not exactly your best buddy."

"Not since I pulled him off your face back in sixth grade," I said.

"Yeah, but you didn't have to beat him up after that."

"I try to look after my friends."

"Maybe if I solve this thing I can pay you back," Micro said. "But there must be somebody we're not thinking of. So far, this doesn't add up to anything."

"How about Mr. Van Woort?" I asked. "Cheryl says that he's taking a computer course."

"Well, he could get at Connor's machine with no problem, but.... Nah. We need someone else who'd have some keys to that room."

"I've got it," I shouted. I felt like someone had just turned on the lights in my brain.

"Got what?"

"I've got the person with the key—I'm sure of it."

"Well, who is it?" Micro asked me.

"Just follow me. Sometimes when a brainer like you gets stumped, a dumb guy like me can still pop up with the answer."

# CHAPTER
# 8

I raced up the stairs to the library as fast as I could. Micro followed behind me. He moved a lot faster than I thought his tiny legs could carry him. Micro is a lot smaller than I am, but he's really stocky. He looks like a midget wrestler now that the weight lifting has made him so strong.

"What do you want in the library?" he asked.

"Cheryl."

"I thought you got shot down by her last year."

"Don't play dumb, Micro," I told him.

"I want to see Cheryl because she's got a master key."

Micro looked at me with a big grin. My brainstorm was the first real break we'd had since all this began.

In a few seconds we were just outside the big glass walls of the library.

And we both stopped cold.

"Who's that on the computer?" Micro whispered to me.

"I can't tell," I whispered back. "Get back against the lockers until we can see who they are. And don't let Cheryl see you, no matter what."

It was so quiet that I was afraid our breathing would give us away. There were three guys back on the far wall, gathered around the computer. We still couldn't see who they were. But I could tell by the size of them that they were no minor players.

Micro and I waited in a space between two banks of lockers. We kept our eyes glued to the guys at the computer. I had a hunch that the three of them were the answer to our problem.

At last, one of the guys turned around to say something to Cheryl. I didn't hear

the words, but I knew the face right
away.

"It's Animal."

"Rob, sometimes your luck is better
than my brains," Micro told me. "I bet
the guy on the computer is Nick Bistas.
Now who could the other one be?"

No sooner had Micro whispered the
question than we had an answer. The
other two turned around and we could
see them—the one at the keyboard was
Nick, all right, and the other was Eric
Weiner.

"Who's that guy?" Micro asked me.

"My next-door neighbor—Animal's brother."

"And your dad wants you to be like him?"

"Hey, it's no joke, Micro. That kid got to college because he's so good on computers."

"Well, I have a hunch he's not doing homework right now. In fact, the three of them look like the kind of gang that might be into computer crime."

"So you think we've caught three hackers, eh?"

"I'll go down to the computer room and tap into the library machine to see what they're up to. Rob, this could be the break we need."

*Or it could be one more false alarm*, I thought.

"You wait here while I go downstairs," Micro said. "Don't let those guys turn off the machine until I get back to you."

With that, Micro left our hiding spot and went down the stairway. He was gone by the time I stopped to think. How was I supposed to stop them from turning off the machine? There were three of them and only one of me. And Animal is our biggest fullback. Me—I'm the smallest quarterback in the league.

I watched them for fifteen minutes. All that time, I wondered how long Micro would take. Up in the library, it was quiet. Then Cheryl looked at her watch and said something to the others. She got up and flipped off two of the overhead lights.

Nick said something back. He had a look on his face like a guy who hadn't quite finished what he wanted to do.

I was afraid that he might turn the computer off right then. If he did, we'd never find out what he was doing on it.

Micro wasn't around, so it was all up to me. In a second, I burst through the library door and surprised them all.

The question was—what was I supposed to do now?

# CHAPTER

# 9

We all stared at each other. Somebody had to make a move, but I didn't know what move to make.

"The library is closing, Rob," Cheryl said.

"Yeah, but only when I show up," I threw back at her.

"Watch how you talk to my girlfriend," Nick said. He got up from the computer and walked toward me.

At least he couldn't turn the machine off when he wasn't near it.

"Sorry about that," I said, smiling. I just wanted to stall for time. Besides, I didn't like the odds of one-against-four.

"Funny seeing *you* here, Eric," I said.

"I came to help Nick with a small program," he said quickly.

"Oh, I bet," I told him. "That must be how Nick got his 92 from Old Mrs. Connor."

"I got mine the same way you got your 38, Rob," Nick broke in.

"How'd you know I got a 38?" I asked him. "The only person I told my grade to was Micro and he wouldn't tell you."

"Lucky guess," Nick said, smiling at me and trying to cover up.

"You know what I think, Nick?" I said, moving between the three of them and the computer. "I think you've busted Connor's code. And I think you've been playing around with the grades. And I think you've moved some money out of the student council accounts and made it look like I did it."

I took a quick look at the computer when I got in front of it. There were the student council files on the screen. My guesses had been right.

"Nick, he knows—" Eric began, shooting a look at Bistas.

"He doesn't know anything—all he's got is a bunch of wild guesses," Nick said, turning to me. "You just want somebody else to take the rap for that missing thousand."

"How'd you know it was a thousand?" I asked him.

Eric looked like he wanted to die on the spot. Animal was all confused. Nick was getting angry. He was caught by his own words—and he knew it.

"A little bird told me, Rob," Nick said, taking a step toward me. "You can't pin the thing on us, anyhow. Who would ever believe that two dumb football players pulled off a computer crime?"

Where was Micro when I needed him? Nick was confessing the whole thing—but there was no one to hear him.

"So you admit it?" I asked him.

"We don't admit nothin'," Animal broke in. "You ain't got proof."

"That's right," Eric said, looking less upset than before. "You can't prove a thing. You can't even prove that you saw me here in the library."

The three of them began to laugh and that made me mad. The problem when I get mad is that I make really stupid mistakes.

"I've got the proof right here," I said, pointing to the computer.

"Nick, you left the student council files on screen!" Eric snapped.

"Relax," Nick said, "we'll just turn the machine off and all his proof goes—poof."

"Over my dead body," I said.

"Is that a threat or a promise?" Nick asked, and the three of them laughed.

"I'm ready for you," I said. I was trying to sound like I could take on all of them.

"O.K., Animal, give him a taste of some real muscle," Nick said. "This is just a hint of what the team will do to you when they find out the uniform money is gone."

Animal came at me. He was big, but he was slow. I threw a flying tackle that brought him to the floor like a giant fish flopping into a boat.

For some reason I thought that Animal would just lay still and play dead. Fat chance! In a second he rolled onto his side and tried to get to his feet. I couldn't let that happen. I jumped on top

of him, pushing him over before he could get up.

✓Where was Micro? Animal was almost twice my size. Even if I could keep him down, one of the others could easily flip off the computer.

Animal got up on one knee and I had to jump him again—but this time he was ready. He grabbed me as I fell on him and twisted me over on the floor.

Now he was on top and I was underneath. I swear he must have weighed as much as a small car. I pushed and shoved and kicked, but I couldn't get free.

The others just laughed. "Don't hurt him too much," Nick said.

"I'm gonna kill him," Animal grunted from on top of me.

I was afraid of that so I struggled against him even more. I tried to pound my knees into him, but that didn't work. Then I tried to grab his hair. This had gone too far to be a fair fight. All I wanted to do was to stay alive a little longer.

Animal started to press his arm across my neck so I couldn't breathe. I

tried to break the hold by hitting his
arm. But that didn't work. There was
only one thing left.

I bit him.

"You dirty pig!" he shouted at me. I
didn't have enough breath left to argue
the point. Animal was so surprised by the
bite that I was able to wiggle free.

I was just getting to my feet when
things got worse. Nick hit me right in
the eye.

Nick's blow set me falling to the floor
and then Animal was on top of me again.
No more wrestling for him. He was just

going to punch my face until it was flat as a pancake. I felt his first punch connect with my jaw, but I couldn't bring up my arms to protect myself.

There was nothing I could do—no way that I could stop him. I braced myself for punch number two, but it never came. Somehow, Animal went flying off me.

# CHAPTER

# 10

When I got to my feet, I saw Animal
twisting on the floor, knocking books all
over the place.

Micro Man was on top of him,
twisting his arm. Animal kept screaming
for Micro to stop.

"All right, let him go," I heard from
the door. It was Old Mrs. Connor.

Micro let go of Animal's arm, but not
before he gave it one last twist.

"He broke it—he broke my arm!"
Animal cried.

"No I didn't, you nerd," Micro told
him. He picked his glasses up off the

floor and then turned to me. "Why didn't you wait for me?"

"He was going to clear the screen," I said. "I just tried to stop him."

"You could have saved yourself the fight," Micro told me. "We have the whole thing copied on disk downstairs."

I felt my swollen eye and wondered why Micro's words of wisdom always came too late to do any good. "So I wrestled with these guys for nothing?"

"Well, if you need a workout, why not try lifting weights?"

"All right, Melvin," Mrs. Connor said. It was always strange to hear someone use Animal's real name. "Stop crying about your arm and tell me how you got into all this. I want a straight story from each of you."

"I told him not to do it," Animal said. "I didn't know about the money until after they did it."

"Who's *they*?" Micro asked.

Animal looked at Nick for a second, then stopped talking.

"All right, Nick, I guess it's your turn to talk," Mrs. Connor said. "It was the three of you, wasn't it?"

Nick nodded yes.

"Who set up the program to break the code?" she asked.

"It was me," Eric said, embarrassed more than the rest of them. "It all started as a game. We were going to give the thousand back after we had a little fun with Rob, that's all. The money is still in the bank. We didn't touch any of it—just moved it to a new account. I can prove it if you give me a chance."

"I'm surprised a fine student like you would get into something like this," Mrs. Connor said.

"It was just a joke at first," Nick broke in. "We were in here one night to pick up Cheryl. And we were goofing around. I told Eric that you kept your grades downstairs on the computer. And he said that he could bust in and change some of the grades around just for a laugh. We dared him to try it. Then we all went down to the computer room just so he could prove how easy it was. That's how it all started."

"But not how it finished," Mrs. Connor said in a stern voice. "How did you get into my classroom?"

The three of them looked at Cheryl. It was Nick who laid the blame. "She's got a key."

"You might as well tell me what you did, Cheryl," Mrs. Connor said, staring hard at her.

"I thought it was a stupid joke right from the start," Cheryl said. "I only gave them the key because the three of them kept bugging me. I didn't have anything else to do with it."

"But you knew about the thousand dollars," I said.

"That was only a joke, Rob. They were

going to give it back right after you got in hot water over the missing money."

"Oh, for sure," I said. Why would they risk giving themselves away to give back the money? It just didn't make sense. "Whose idea was it to blame it on me?" I asked.

"We had to blame it on somebody," Eric said. "When Nick saw that we could pin it on you . . . well, so much the better. Nick wanted to get even with you and your friend for something back in sixth grade. Believe me—we were going to give the money back."

"And my name is Santa Claus," I told him.

"All right, Rob, I know you're upset, but take it easy," Mrs. Connor said. "I think we've gone about as far on this as we can right now. I want to see all of you in the office on Monday morning. Nick, Cheryl, and Mel—you better bring your parents. I'm not sure whether the principal will bring in the police, but I can tell you now that you won't get off easy."

"What about us?" Micro asked her.

"I'm still not happy about the way you

86

broke into my file, young man. But I think I'll let you off if you help me set up a new computer code. One that nobody can break into," Mrs. Connor said, looking at Micro.

"And Rob, you had better get cleaned up and get some rest. Mark tells me that you were the one who solved this mess. I have a hunch that the principal might want to shake your hand Monday morning."

# CHAPTER

# 11

The principal really did shake my hand on Monday. Mrs. Varey said she had always trusted me. She was glad to see me in the clear.

I wasn't in the office when she dealt with Nick and the others. From what I hear, there weren't any handshakes.

Even though they gave the money back, Mrs. Varey felt the whole thing was very serious. Nick was kicked out of school for two weeks and dropped from all sports for the year. Animal got the same two weeks off, but he never came back. I hear he has some sort of cruddy job out west. Animal's brother, Eric, got off with a warning and a letter to his school. It seemed funny that the brains behind the whole thing should get off the easiest. Maybe that's how crime works.

Cheryl ended up losing her job at the library. She blamed Nick for that, but I think she should have blamed herself. People are like that.

Micro helped Mrs. Connor put a new code on the school files. He says that his new system is really safe. Even *he* can't break into it. But Micro's kid brother is working right now on a way to bust the new system. The kid says he just wants to show that it can be done. That's what all hackers say. One of these days Micro should sit down with the kid. Somebody has got to tell him all the trouble he can get into.

The new football uniforms came in last week. The football team has been treating me like a hero for getting them. They weren't quite so nice to Nick Bistas when they found out what he had tried to do.

Micro doesn't help me in computers any more. I think I should learn about them by myself. I may not be quite the whiz kid that he is, but I'm no dummy.

My dad has gotten off my back lately. When the news came out about Eric Weiner, my dad must have felt lucky to have me. I think my father's starting to see that there's more to a person than brains. I'm even starting to see that myself. When Micro starts acting like he's so far above me, I cut him down. After all, I was the one who solved the crime.

Things are more equal between us now. Micro knows he doesn't owe me a thing any more. Ever since sixth grade, he felt he owed me a favor for pulling Nick Bistas off his face. Now that he pulled Animal off mine, we're even.

In fact, I found out that I'm not too far behind him in our computer grades.

"I've got some good news for you," Micro told me just two days ago.

"Yeah?"

"I went back through the grades in computer class and found out what happened."

"It was that lousy project grade that made me bomb out."

"No, it was Nick Bistas who bombed the project," he said. "They switched the project grades around and then added points to Nick's grade."

"So?"

"So your mid-term grade in computers should have been a 74."

"Really?"

"I wouldn't kid you about something like that," Micro said.

"And what about your grade?" I asked him.

"Mrs. Connor says she'll give me some bonus points for setting up the new code.

That should give me a 99 on the final report."

"Why can't she give you a hundred?"

"Because no one's perfect," Micro said, "not even a human computer."

## About the Author

Paul Kropp lives in Hamilton, Ontario with his wife, Marsha, and their three sons. He began writing the books in the **Encounters Series** in 1978 while teaching special education at a local high school. He now has over a quarter million books in print, all dealing with the concerns of young adults.

If you enjoyed this book, you might also enjoy reading . . .

## BURN OUT
Bob and Chewie have a plan to catch the firebugs on Maple Street. The plan seems good at first. But when it backfires, they get trapped in the basement of a burning house.

## DEAD ON
What is making the strange noises in the hall outside Larry's room? It can't be a ghost. Larry doesn't believe in ghosts. But someone—or something—keeps leading him to the attic of the old house.

## DIRT BIKE
Forty cycles roar out of the start chute. Randy races toward the first turn on his yellow dirt bike. He looks over at Bozo and grits his teeth. Only one of them can come out the winner.

## HOT CARS
At first Robert doesn't know who is killing his dogs or wrecking his father's truck. When he gets trapped by a stolen-car gang, the answer almost kills him.

## WILD ONE
Kate saves Wild One from Banner's whip and gets to train the horse herself. But that's only a start. Can she prove he can race before it's too late?

How many books in the **Encounters Series** have you read?

AMY'S WISH
BABY, BABY
BURN OUT
DEAD ON
DIRT BIKE
DOPE DEAL
FAIR PLAY
GANG WAR
HOT CARS
MICRO MAN
NO WAY
RUNAWAY
SNOW GHOST
SPIN OUT
THE BEAST
WILD ONE